Native
American
Peoples

SIOUX

D. L. Birchfield

Gareth Stevens Publishing
A WORLD ALMANAC EDUCATION GROUP COMPANY

Please visit our web site at: www.garethstevens.com
For a free color catalog describing Gareth Stevens Publishing's list of high-quality books
and multimedia programs, call 1-800-542-2595 (USA) or 1-800-387-3178 (Canada).
Gareth Stevens Publishing's fax: (414) 332-3567.

Library of Congress Cataloging-in-Publication Data

Birchfield, D. L., 1948-
Sioux / by D. L. Birchfield.
    p. cm. — (Native American peoples)
    Summary: A discussion of the history, culture, and contemporary life of the
Sioux Indians.
    Includes bibliographical references and index.
    ISBN 0-8368-3669-3 (lib. bdg.)
    1. Dakota Indians—History—Juvenile literature. 2. Dakota Indians—Social
life and customs—Juvenile literature. [1. Dakota Indians.] I. Title. II. Series.
E99.D1B57   2003
978.004'9752—dc21   2002191132

First published in 2003 by
Gareth Stevens Publishing
A World Almanac Education Group Company
330 West Olive Street, Suite 100
Milwaukee, WI 53212 USA

Produced by Discovery Books
Project editor: Valerie J. Weber
Designer and page production: Sabine Beaupré
Photo researcher: Valerie J. Weber
Native American consultant: Robert J. Conley, M.A., Former Director of Native American
    Studies at Morningside College and Montana State University
Maps and diagrams: Stefan Chabluk
Gareth Stevens editorial direction: Mark Sachner
Gareth Stevens art direction: Tammy Gruenewald
Gareth Stevens production: Jessica L. Yanke

Photo credits: AP/Wide World Photos: cover, pp. 10 (top), 20, 23, 25, 27; North Wind Picture
Archives: pp. 5, 8 (top), 13, 14, 15, 16 (top), 17; SuperStock, Inc.: pp. 6, 18, 21; Corbis: p. 7;
National Park Service, Little Bighorn Battlefield National Monument: pp. 8 (bottom), 9, 10
(bottom), 11; Courtesy of the Library of Congress: pp. 12, 16 (bottom); © Mary Annette
Pember: 22, 26; © Tiffany Midge: p. 24.

Printed in the United States of America

1 2 3 4 5 6 7 8 9 07 06 05 04 03

Cover: An Oglala Sioux elder holds a presidential peace medallion given to Indian leaders by
the Lewis and Clark expedition.

Contents

Words that appear in the glossary are printed in
boldface type the first time they appear in the text.

Origins

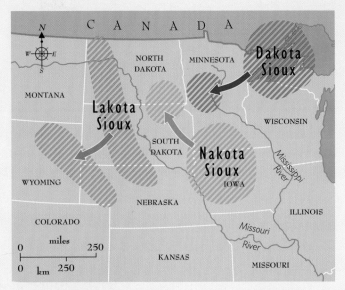

This map shows the Sioux groups and their movement from their former territories as they were pushed farther west.

Sioux Country

The Sioux are one of the largest Native American nations, with a total population in the tens of thousands. Their homelands once covered the woodlands of the upper Mississippi River Valley, in what is now Minnesota, Wisconsin, Iowa, and Illinois. Today, they live on reservations in South and North Dakota, Minnesota, and Montana and throughout the United States and Canada.

No one knows exactly when the Sioux and other Native American tribes entered North America. Like most Native cultures, the Sioux have, for centuries, told an origin story that explains how they came to live here. According to the Sioux elders, they came from the Star Nation to a place beneath the earth and emerged from Wind Cave in the Black Hills of present-day South Dakota. The Black Hills, which they call *Paha Sapa,* "the heart of everything that is," are a sacred place for the Sioux.

Various scientific **theories** try to explain how the Sioux and other Native peoples arrived in North America. The main theory is that the ancestors of today's Native Americans came from Asia during the Ice Age over a land mass across the Bering Strait between North America and Asia. Another theory suggests that Indians came by boat along the Pacific Ocean from Asia.

French Creek winds its way through a meadow in the Black Hills. The Black Hills are a place of special spiritual significance not only to the Sioux but to other Plains tribes as well, including the Cheyennes.

The Sioux Languages

The Siouan language family is one of the most widely distributed throughout the eastern half of North America and includes tribes that are not called Sioux. Depending upon which of the three main dialects, or forms, of the language they speak, the Sioux call themselves Lakotas (also called the Tetons), Nakotas (or Yanktons), or Dakotas (or Santees). Each of the three main divisions of the Sioux nation includes a number of subtribes.

"Sioux" itself is a word from the **Ojibwe** language meaning "adders," a kind of poisonous snake. (The Sioux did not always get along well with their Ojibwe neighbors.)

Lakota Words

Lakota	Pronunciation	English
kola	ko-lah	friend
toka	toe-kah	enemy
wakan	wah-con	sacred
wi	we	sun
wicasa	we-kah-sah	man
sa	sah	red
mato	mah-toe	bear
wicoti	we-koh-tee	camp
hunka	hun-kah	parent
oyate	o-yah-tay	people
winyan	win-yon	woman

Chapter 2

History

The Beginning of Conflict

The Sioux did not have much early contact with Europeans. By the late 1600s, however, the Ojibwes had traded with the French for guns, and they began using those weapons to push the Sioux tribes out of the woodlands of the upper Mississippi River Valley west onto the northern Great Plains.

The Lakota Sioux were pushed the farthest west, all the way to the plains in present-day Wyoming, western South Dakota, and western Nebraska. The Nakotas settled mostly on the northern plains in the present-day states of North and South Dakota. The Dakotas settled along the far western edge of their old homeland, mostly in present-day western Minnesota.

Nineteenth-century **media** depicted the West as wide-open spaces ripe for settlement, as shown in this 1861 painting *The Way of the Empire Is Going Westward,* by Emanuel Leutze. The European-Americans, however, found the land had long been inhabited by Native peoples.

The Settlers Arrive

In 1804, as Meriwether Lewis and William Clark began their journey of exploration across the continent, they visited some Lakota villages along the Missouri River. They were to be followed by many more Americans; between the 1840s and the completion of the **transcontinental** railroad in 1869, nearly 400,000 Americans passed through the southern edge of the Sioux country on the wagon trail to Utah and the West Coast known as the Oregon Trail. In a **treaty** with the United States in 1851, the Sioux agreed to allow the travelers to use the trail.

In 1854, however, a dispute over a cow that had wandered away from a wagon train caused a foolish young U.S. Army officer, Lieutenant John Grattan, to fire a cannon into a Lakota village, killing the village chief. The enraged Lakotas then killed the officer and all twenty-eight of his men. The next year, the army struck back by destroying a Lakota village, killing about seventy people.

That same year, 1854, the Dakotas went to war against settlers who were taking their land in Minnesota. In 1862, when the long, bloody war was over, the United States government hanged thirty-eight Dakotas in the largest mass execution in U.S. history, and the Dakotas lost most of their Minnesota land.

Young Crazy Horse

A model of the Crazy Horse Memorial in front of the mountaintop in the Black Hills that is being carved in its likeness.

Among the Indians who witnessed the fight over the cow was a young Lakota who would later be known as Crazy Horse, one of the greatest Sioux military leaders. He was only about fourteen years old at the time, not yet a warrior, but the terrible event made a lasting impression on him. He never trusted the U.S. Army again.

War on the Plains

In the mid-1860s, gold seekers began streaming through the heart of Lakota country to get to a gold strike at present-day Bozeman, Montana. Over the protests of the Sioux, the U.S. Army built three forts along the Bozeman Trail to protect the miners. The Sioux went to war. Led by Red Cloud, they attacked the forts. A young war leader, Crazy Horse, gained fame in December 1866, when he trapped and killed a **cavalry** troop of about eighty men. In 1868, under the Fort Laramie Treaty with the Sioux, the United States abandoned the three forts. The Sioux burned them down in a great victory celebration.

The 1868 Fort Laramie Treaty also stated that the Black Hills in South Dakota belonged to the Sioux. In 1874, however, the U.S. Army

Red Cloud led his people in wars against the Pawnees and Crows and battled the United States in the 1860s.

Lieutenant Colonel George Armstrong Custer's expedition into the Black Hills in 1874. Custer knew that he was violating the 1868 Fort Laramie treaty by entering the Black Hills without the permission of the Sioux, but he had no respect for the rights of the Indians.

A photo taken in 1879, of the Little Bighorn battle site, three years after Custer's defeat. Horse bones and boots are scattered on the hillside.

deliberately violated the treaty when Lieutenant Colonel George Custer confirmed rumors of gold in the Black Hills, starting a wild gold rush into the heart of the sacred land of the Sioux. The Sioux went to war again.

Victory and Defeat

With their main leader Crazy Horse, the Sioux and their Cheyenne allies won a stunning victory at the Battle of the Rosebud against a large army. A few days later, on June 25, 1876, at the Battle of the Little Bighorn, they killed Lieutenant Colonel Custer and all of his men, stunning the nation.

The United States sent out large armies and within a year forced all of the Sioux and Cheyennes to surrender. Meanwhile, independent buffalo hunters, with the help of the U.S. Army, were **slaughtering** the buffalo herds for their hides. Without the animal they depended on, the Sioux lost much of their way of life and were forced to accept life on **reservations** mostly in North and South Dakota.

Crazy Horse rode up . . . [and said] "There's a good fight coming over the hill." I looked where he pointed and saw Custer and his blue-coats pouring over the hill. I thought there were a million of them. "That's where the big fight is going to be," said Crazy Horse. . . . He was not a bit excited. He made a joke of it.

Short Buffalo, Lakota

This Ghost Dance shirt was returned to the tribe in 1999 from a museum in Scotland.

The Ghost Dance

Despair at the misery of reservation life led the Sioux to embrace a new religion that swept through the reservations in 1890. The Ghost Dance religion was founded by a Paiute prophet named Wovoka. He preached that, if Indians embraced the Ghost Dance, the buffalo would return, along with all the dead Indians, and the white people would disappear.

On the Sioux reservations, some religious leaders said that special Ghost Dance shirts would protect them from bullets. The army became alarmed when the influential leader, Sitting Bull, embraced the new religion.

Sitting Bull

By 1857, when he was in his mid twenties, Sitting Bull was both a **medicine man** and a war chief. After helping to defeat Custer at the Battle of the Little Bighorn, Sitting Bull led his followers to Canada to avoid capture by the U.S. Army. Exhaustion and a lack of food forced him to surrender in 1881 at Fort Buford in Dakota Territory. In his later years, he strongly opposed government efforts to force the Sioux to adopt white values. He was killed during the army's attempt to arrest him.

U.S. soldiers picking up Lakotas killed at the massacre at Wounded Knee. The bodies, frozen in the deep winter cold, were buried in a mass grave.

Wounded Knee, 1890

Ghost Dance followers gathered at a place called the Stronghold in the Black Hills. Big Foot, an influential chief who did not embrace the new religion, gathered his three hundred people and rushed across the Dakotas in the middle of winter toward the Stronghold to try to stop war from breaking out. He wanted to talk everyone into remaining calm.

The army, unaware that Big Foot was trying to encourage peace, sent troops to intercept him. Soldiers surrounded Big Foot's band in late December 1890 as they were camped along Wounded Knee Creek. When the army tried to take all the band's rifles, a gun went off. No one knows who fired the shot. The army fired its cannons, killing at least 150 of the mostly unarmed men, women, and children. The dead were buried in a mass grave, and the Sioux **reluctantly** resigned themselves to reservation life.

As part of the U.S. government's plan to make the Sioux adopt European-American ways, the Sioux were taught how to be farmers.

Reservation Life and Acculturation

Late-nineteenth-century Americans believed there was no place in their society for Indians to remain Indians — the reservation system was designed to force Indians to abandon their culture, language, religion, and **economy**. The government attempted to force them to adopt white values in a process called **acculturation**. It was a grim time for the Sioux.

[The Sioux] understood that ample provisions would be made for their support; instead, their supplies have been reduced and much of the time they have been living on half and two-thirds rations.

General Nelson A. Miles, U.S. Army, 1891

People in the U.S. government who were supposed to help Native Americans did just the opposite. With the buffalo herds gone, the only food for the Sioux was what the U.S. government provided at the reservation, where the Indian agent was the government's official representative. Some Indian agents took money meant for food and offered cheap, spoiled beef and flour filled with insects to the people on their reservations, pocketing the money they had saved.

The American Indian Movement

The traditional Sioux ways of governing themselves were no longer allowed. Poverty, unemployment, poor health, and high death rates on the Sioux reservations made them islands of despair.

By the 1970s, Indians from across the country were determined to change the conditions on their reservations. A number of young Sioux became members of the American Indian Movement (AIM) and traveled to Washington, D.C., in what became known as "The Trail of Broken Treaties." They seized and occupied the headquarters of the Bureau of Indian Affairs, bringing media attention to Indian problems.

Similar events around the country forced the U.S government to take action. Particularly important were laws to allow Native Americans freedom of religion, which helped usher in a new era for the Sioux and other Indians.

The cruelest part of acculturation was the off-reservation boarding school system. Sioux children were taken by force from their families and sent to boarding schools. Forbidden to speak their language, they were forced to learn English.

Traditional Way of Life

A Plains Indian village on the move, using the travois, a horse-drawn sled. Moving an entire village was a great undertaking, requiring the help and cooperation of everyone.

A People of the Horse

After the Sioux acquired horses from other tribes (that had gotten them from the Spanish) during the 1700s, their world changed dramatically. Horses made travel easier. Before the horse, dogs had been used to drag tent poles and **tepees** across the plains. On a pole sled commonly known as a **travois**, horses could drag those items much farther and faster than dogs, and they could move much more weight. Entire villages of people and all their goods could be moved easily and quickly.

An Indian horse race. Horses had great value for Plains Indians, for recreation as well as transportation, war, and moving villages.

An Improving Lifestyle

Thanks to the horse, the Sioux's quality of life improved during the eighteenth century. Tepee poles could be longer, and the tepees bigger. Hunting buffalo became much easier and more efficient. Because food was easier to get, more babies lived to become adults. As both their ability to travel and their population increased, so did their power.

The era of warfare on foot gave way to one that produced some of the most spectacular light cavalry in history. Much of Sioux warfare, however, consisted simply of horse-stealing raids against other tribes. It was a way for young men to prove themselves and to gain wealth and honor within the tribe.

Lakotas on Horseback

The Lakotas, especially, took to the horse as if they had been born to ride. The traditional Indian style of child rearing, in which children are pretty much allowed to do whatever they think they can do, produced a culture where children barely more than toddlers performed breathtaking feats of horsemanship. By the time they were teens, they had amazing riding skills.

Horses, rifles, and pistols made it possible for the buffalo to be killed in great numbers. However, it was the coming of the railroads that made it possible for commercial hunters to hunt the buffalo nearly to extinction.

A People of the Buffalo

For the Sioux, especially the Lakotas, moving to the Great Plains made them a people of the buffalo, a great change from the woodland people they once had been. The Great Plains were home to immense herds of buffalo — at their greatest number estimated to be 75 million animals. The Plains also teemed with

many other kinds of animals, including elk and deer. It was a paradise for a people skilled at harvesting the plants and animals that lived around them.

The buffalo provided for nearly every Sioux need — not just for food, but for clothing and shelter as well. Buffalo robes warmed their beds on cold winter nights. Buffalo hides, stitched together with buffalo **sinew**, made a strong tent fabric, able to withstand rain and cold winter winds.

When draped around a framework of long, slender poles, the buffalo hides formed a tepee, a home that could be quickly put together or taken down and easily carried.

The Sioux fashioned buffalo horns into spoons and large bones into weapons. They cut tanned hides into thin strips and wound the strips into stout ropes. They made glue by boiling the hooves.

A buffalo hunt was an occasion for a great feast. One buffalo, weighing a ton or more, provided more fresh meat than could be eaten at one time. The remaining meat was cut into strips and dried in the sun, making a **jerky** that would last a long time.

～ww～ The Slaughter of the Buffalo Herds ～ww～

The end of the buffalo herds — within little more than a decade around the 1870s — came so suddenly as to stagger the imagination. The slaughter followed railroad building, offering hide hunters a means of transporting hides, which sold for about a dollar each back east. The hunters

Before the Plains Indians acquired horses, killing a buffalo was a difficult task. Getting close enough to a buffalo to kill it with an arrow required great skill.

took only the hides, leaving the meat to rot on the Plains. The U.S. Army encouraged the slaughter as one way of ending the Plains Indians' way of life and forcing them onto the reservation.

The slaughter began in Kansas in the early 1870s, wiping out the herds there by 1873. By 1875, the Texas herds had been killed. The railroads reached Montana in 1871, and by 1875, the northern herds were gone. With the slaughter of the buffalo herds, the Plains Indian way of life disappeared.

In the era of the buffalo, during the seventeenth and eighteenth centuries, the basic unit of Sioux political organization was the *tiyospaye*. Each tiyospaye consisted of about thirty or more households of related families. The families of the tiyospaye traveled together, hunted together, and spent the entire year together. At intervals, all of the many tiyospayes in the tribe would come together for a large meeting of the entire tribe.

A nineteenth-century painting by Seth Eastman showing Sioux men in council. The Sioux place great value on the wisdom of their elders, and their traditional government is designed to allow the people to be guided by that wisdom.

Tribal Leaders

Each tiyospaye had a headman who achieved and kept his position by virtue of his character. He could lose that position by making foolish decisions, putting the group in danger, or failing to live up to the high standards expected of him. While he was not elected, the people had to agree to let him lead.

The most able and respected headmen from the tiyospayes were admitted into male societies called *nacas*. The most important of these societies was called the *Naca Omincia,* which was very much like a national council, having the power to make war and peace. From among its members, *wicasa itancans* (executive officers) were appointed to carry out the decisions of the Naca Omincia.

The *wicasa wakan,* or medicine man, holds a special place in traditional Sioux life, both historically and today. He is a healer, respected for his power to cure, as well as a wise leader.

Today, large extended families still have leaders among them who act as an informal kind of traditional Sioux government. This form of government is not recognized by the United States government, and that causes many of the problems between the U.S. government and the Sioux today — and among the Sioux themselves, between those who follow the old ways and those who don't.

∿∿∿ The Qualities of a Leader ∿∿∿

Traditionally, people have become leaders among the Sioux by having characteristics that are valued by the community. These include wisdom, courage, generosity, compassion for the needs of others, and an ability to gain spiritual guidance from dreams and visions.

An Oglala Sioux man visiting Bear Butte, in the Black Hills, a holy site for the Sioux. The prayer ribbons on the trees represent religious commitments made by the visitors to the sacred ground.

> The world was a library and its books were the stones, leaves, grass, brooks and the birds and animals that shared, alike with us, the storms and blessings of the earth. We learn to do what only the student of nature ever learns, and that is to feel beauty. We never rail at the storms, the furious, winds, the biting frosts and snows. Bright days and dark days are both expressions of the Great Mystery.
>
> *Luther Standing Bear, an Oglala Sioux*

Beliefs and Values

Sioux traditional religious beliefs remain strong, even today. Traditionally, the Sioux believe in a Creator, sometimes called the Great Mystery. They believe that the Great Mystery is present in all things on the earth, including the rocks, trees, animals, water and wind. They seek guidance from the Creator in dreams and visions and place great importance on trying to live in harmony with other people. Medicine men help interpret the dreams and visions.

For the Sioux, Bear Butte in the Black Hills is a place for fasting and praying, somewhere to seek a vision to guide one's life. Unfortunately, Bear Butte is now controlled by the U.S. government. The Sioux must pay fees to the U.S. park rangers to enter Bear Butte. Tourists often show little respect for the prayer ribbons that the Sioux tie to the bushes and the tobacco offerings to the Creator that they leave on the butte. Tobacco is a sacred plant, used in prayers and ceremonies.

The Sun Dance

The most important religious ceremonial, the Sun Dance is held each year in the summer. The ceremonies help the participants cleanse their spirits and renew their vows to work for the welfare of the tribe.

Sioux traditional values emphasize the welfare of the group rather than the individual. Sharing and having concern for others are highly valued. **Hoarding** wealth, by not sharing with others, is frowned upon.

The Sioux Community

The Sioux may be poor, in terms of money, but they share that condition of poverty together. The Sioux value a rich and rewarding family life with their relatives throughout the entire community more than trying to make money. Sioux contentment with this outlook on life and their sense of what is important and what is not important are a measure of how successful they have been at surviving an era when their culture was under threat of extinction.

Sioux performers of the Eagle Dance. Traditional Sioux dances and ceremonies were banned for many years by the U.S. government in its attempt to force the Sioux to adopt white values.

Today

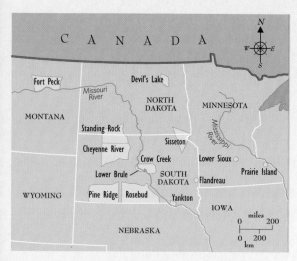

Sioux reservations of various sizes are scattered throughout Minnesota, Montana, and North and South Dakota.

The Contemporary Sioux

Sixteen Sioux reservations lie in the United States. Other Sioux people live in the Prairie Provinces of Canada. Today, about half the Sioux live on the reservations; most of the others live in large cities. Land area, population, tribal divisions represented, natural resources, and economic conditions all vary greatly among the Sioux reservations. An elected tribal council governs each reservation.

Life on most of the reservations is difficult, with many people lacking jobs. Poverty and despair have led to alcohol abuse and poor health. These problems brought violence to the Pine Ridge Reservation in the 1970s, from which the Sioux are still recovering. It was a struggle over

Three-year-old Dakota children at a day care center today. They are sitting in front of a mural that depicts scenes from traditional Dakota life.

which group would control the reservation — the Sioux who want to follow the old ways or the Sioux who have adopted non-Native values. Nearly one hundred traditional Sioux people were killed in the violence. The struggle between those two groups continues today, but it is no longer marked by the violence that made the reservation a dangerous place in the 1970s.

These conflicts brought media attention to Indian problems and helped change U.S. policy. Instead of trying to force Indians to give up their cultures, the government sought ways to allow Indians to have more control over their own lives.

Wounded Knee, 1973

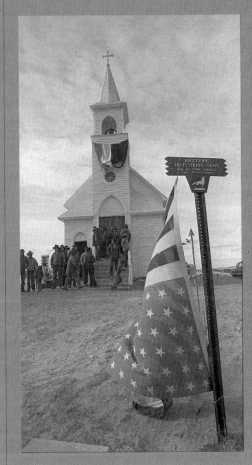

For more than two months in 1973, the American Indian Movement (AIM) occupied the church at Wounded Knee, South Dakota, on the Pine Ridge Reservation, the scene of the 1890 massacre. AIM members held it as the center of an Indian nation — independent of the U.S. government — for seventy-one days. The incident deepened the divisions among the Sioux at Pine Ridge that caused several years of violence over who would control the reservation and speak for the Lakota Sioux tribe.

March 3, 1973, a U.S. flag flies upside down outside Wounded Knee church, on the Pine Ridge Reservation in South Dakota. An upside-down flag is a signal of distress.

Literature and the Arts

Sioux authors, scholars, and visual and performing artists have been leaders in the intellectual and cultural life of American Indians. In the visual and performing arts, Oscar Howe (1915–1984), from the Crow Creek Reservation, became one of the best-known Indian artists in North America. Today, his work is a part of the permanent collection of many museums. Kevin Locke, from the Standing Rock Reservation, is famous nationally as an Indian flute player and hoop dancer. He has performed at the Kennedy Center in Washington, D.C.

Tiffany Midge is one of the most promising young Sioux poets and activists. Her work has been honored by other writers.

Sioux authors have also made important contributions to children's literature. The most acclaimed author, Virginia Driving Hawk Sneve, from the Rosebud Reservation, won the 1992 North American Indian Prose Award.

Vine Deloria, Jr., from the Standing Rock Reservation, is easily the best-known Sioux author. He holds graduate degrees in both law and religious studies. He gained national attention in 1969 with his first book, *Custer Died for Your Sins*, which was published while he was still a student in law school. He has published many other influential books, including *God Is Red*.

The Sioux also have many other authors who publish poetry or fiction, including Susan Powers, Tiffany Midge, Robert L. Perea, Philip H. Red-Eagle, Jr., and Elizabeth Cook-Lynn. Their work is widely used in college courses in Native American literature.

Russell Means

In the 1970s, Russell Means was one of the most active Sioux members of the American Indian Movement. He was a spokesperson for AIM when the activist organization took over the church at Wounded Knee in 1973. In the 1990s, he became a Hollywood actor, starring in major motion pictures. He is best known for his role in the movie *Last Of The Mohicans* but continues to be active in Native political issues.

Russell Means speaks to supporters before beginning his walk across New Mexico in his campaign for governor in 2002.

Current Sioux Issues

In the 1980s, when former professional basketball player Bill Bradley was a United States senator from New Jersey, he conducted a basketball camp one summer for Sioux children on the Pine Ridge Reservation. Seeing their poverty, Senator Bradley asked the children what he could do in the Senate to help them. He was surprised when the children told him that the thing they wanted the most was for the United States to return Paha Sapa (the Black Hills) to them.

Sioux children jumping on a trampoline. Sioux children, like children everywhere, just want to have fun.

Victory, of a Sort

To the Sioux, the Black Hills are their most sacred land. In the twentieth century, they went to court against the U.S. government to have them returned to their care. In proceedings before the U.S. Indian Claims Commission, the Sioux won a decision that the Black Hills had been taken from them illegally. In 1980, however, the Supreme Court ruled that the Sioux were only entitled to money — a $122 million award — not the land itself.

The Sioux have refused to take the money, which has now increased to more than $400 million. They continue to demand that the Black Hills be returned to them.

They point to previous cases. In the 1970s, Congress passed legislation, signed by President Richard Nixon, that returned the sacred Blue Lake to Taos Pueblo in New Mexico, along with 48,000 acres (19,433 ha) of surrounding land. Presently, the only way the Black Hills can be returned to the Sioux is by an act of Congress. In the 1980s, legislation to that effect, sponsored

> We want no white person or persons here. The Black Hills belong to me. If the whites try to take them, I will fight.
>
> *Sitting Bull*

by Senator Bradley, came very close to passing in Congress. The Sioux are not losing faith and continue trying to convince Congress to pass that legislation.

Today, as the twenty-first century begins, the Sioux people still face many problems. But they have also produced many capable leaders who are working hard to solve those problems and to continue their heritage as one of the great Indian nations.

American Indian Movement (AIM) activists Dennis Banks, *left,* and Clyde Bellecourt beat a drum and chant during a rally at the Pine Ridge Reservation in South Dakota.

Time Line

1600s	Ojibwes acquire guns, push the Sioux to the west.
late 1600s and 1700s	Sioux acquire horses.
1804	Lewis and Clark expedition visits Sioux villages.
1840–1869	Thousands of Americans pass through Sioux country on the Oregon Trail.
1851	Sioux sign treaty allowing travelers to use the Oregon Trail.
1854	Dispute over a cow leads to violent clash with U.S. Army.
1856	Army strikes back by destroying a Sioux village.
1862	Thirty-eight Dakotas are hanged at end of Dakota Minnesota conflict.
mid-1860s	War over the Bozeman Trail.
1868	Treaty of Fort Laramie.
1874	Custer leads troops exploring for gold in Black Hills.
1876	Battle of the Rosebud and the Battle of the Little Bighorn.
1877	Crazy Horse killed.
1890	Sitting Bull killed; massacre at Wounded Knee.
late 1800s and 1900s	Despair on reservations over U.S. government policy of acculturation and the off-reservation boarding-school system.
1973	Siege of Wounded Knee.
1974	U.S. Indian Claims Commission awards $122 million to the Sioux Nation for illegal taking of the Black Hills; the Sioux refuse to take the money, which as of 2002 has grown to $400 million
1980	U.S. Supreme Court upholds U.S. Indian Claims Commission money award to the Sioux.
1985	Senator Bill Bradley introduces a bill to give the Black Hills back to the Sioux Nation in the U.S. Senate; Representative James Howard introduces a similar bill in the U.S. House of Representatives. Both bills are voted down.

Glossary

acculturation: the process of forcing one group to adopt the culture — the language, lifestyle, and values — of another.

cavalry: warriors or soldiers trained to fight on horseback.

economy: the way a country or people produces, divides up, and uses its goods and money.

hoarding: keeping something for yourself and not sharing it with others.

jerky: thin strips of meat, dried in the sun, until most of their moisture is removed.

media: television, radio, newspapers, the Internet, and other forms of communication.

medicine man: a spiritual or religious leader.

Mount Rushmore: a monument in the Black Hills featuring large stone carvings of four U.S. presidents.

Ojibwe: also known as Chippewa or Anishinabe (their own name for themselves).

reluctantly: unwillingly.

reservations: land set aside by the U.S. government.

sinew: tendon, a tough, fibrous tissue used for sewing thread.

slaughter: killing, especially in large numbers.

tepee: a cone-shaped tent supported by long, slender pine poles and draped with buffalo hides.

theory: a group of ideas that explain something.

transcontinental: crossing a continent.

travois: a sled consisting of two poles pulled across the ground.

treaty: an agreement among two or more peoples or nations.

More Resources

Web Sites:

www.travelsd.com/history/sioux/sioux.htm Travel guide to the Great Sioux Nation.

www.littlesioux.org A journey into Lakota Sioux culture that includes movies of a powwow and samples of Lakota music.

www.pbs.org/weta/thewest/people/a_c/crazyhorse.htm Contains information about Crazy Horse and links to other Sioux leaders and issues.

Videos:

Incident at Oglala: The Leonard Peltier Story. Live Home Video, 1991.

Paha Sapa: The Struggle for The Black Hills. HBO, 1993.

Wiping the Tears of Seven Generations. Kifaru Productions, 1992.

Books:

Bial, Raymond. *The Sioux* (Lifeways). Marshall Cavendish Corp., 1998.

Eastman, Charles Alexander, and Elaine Goodale Eastman. *Wigwam Evenings: 27 Sioux Folktales*. Dover Publications, 2000.

Guttmacher, Peter. *Crazy Horse: Sioux War Chief* (North American Indians of Achievement). Chelsea House, 1994.

Kavasch, E. Barrie. *Lakota Sioux Children and Elders Talk Together*. Powerkids Press, 1999.

Rinaldi, Ann. *My Heart Is on the Ground: The Diary of Nannie Little Rose, a Sioux Girl, Carlisle Indian School, Pennsylvania, 1880* (Dear America). Scholastic Paperbacks, 1999.

Santella, Andrew. *The Lakota Sioux* (True Book). Children's Press, 2001.

Todd, Anne M. *The Sioux: People of the Great Plains* (American Indian Nations). Bridgestone Books, 2002.

Things to Think About and Do

What Difference Do Horses Make?

Draw pictures showing how life would be for the Sioux on the buffalo plains both before and after they acquired horses. What would a buffalo hunt look like with horses and without them? How would moving a village from one camp to another look different?

What Should Be Done about the Black Hills?

The U.S. Indian Claims Commission ruled that the United States took the Black Hills from the Sioux illegally. What do you think the United States should do about the Black Hills? Should U.S. citizens today feel responsible for things the government did in the past? How should future generations try to solve problems from the past? Write an essay with your thoughts.

Drawing Daily Life

Draw pictures showing all of the things the Sioux were able to make from a buffalo for use in their daily life. Decorate the tepees and clothing with painted symbols, beads, and porcupine quills. Look at the photos in this book for ideas about how to decorate the items.

Index